The Ghosts who Danced

and other spooky stories
from around the world

Saviour Pirotta
Illustrated by **Paul Hess**

Contents

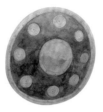

The Ghost Ship
A STORY FROM RHODE ISLAND, USA

Hans had never seen such a magnificent schooner before. *The Palatine* – a British ship sailing out of Rotterdam in Holland. Its masts stood tall and straight, its sails waiting to be unfurled. People were swarming up the gangplank, mostly families hoping to start a new life in America.

"Well, Hans," said his mother, standing on the quay. "What a fine ship to be sailing on, to be sure. Your father will be very proud when he comes home from his own travels and hears about it. You be a good cabin boy, now. Make sure you say your prayers every night, and bring your mama something pretty from America."

"I will, Mama." Hans hugged his mother goodbye and hurried up the gangplank, his haversack bouncing against his shoulders.

The Palatine was teeming with activity. There were sailors getting ready to pull up anchor and passengers, rich and poor, settling into their cabins for the long journey. The hold was full of precious cargo packed in large wooden chests, tied securely in place with thick rope.

It was the first time Hans had been to sea but he had no trouble finding his sea legs. All the men in his family had been sailors and Hans was determined to follow in their footsteps. The crew liked him right away and he soon learnt how to look after the captain, polishing his shoes, powdering his wig, dusting the cabin and fetching his meals from the galley.

The Palatine sailed bravely across the ocean, fighting her way through choppy seas, waiting patiently when there was no wind to fill her sails. And then, as luck would have it, a terrible storm arose. Many passengers were swept overboard, never to reach America. To make matters worse, the water in the barrels turned sour and more people died drinking it, including the captain. The first mate took command of the ship, and a hard taskmaster he was too. Hans was run off his feet, fetching and carrying, making sure the new captain's cabin was shipshape.

Then, late one evening, the coast of America appeared on the horizon, a brown line as thin as a piece of string.

That night the ship's carpenter shook Hans awake in his hammock. "Do ye wanna be rich, lad?"

"I'm sorry?" said Hans.

"Do ye wanna be rich?" repeated the carpenter in a hoarse whisper. "Do ye want to go home laden with gold for your ma, or do ye want to spend the rest of your life emptying the captain's chamber pot?"

"I'm not sure what you mean," replied Hans.

"We're near in America," said the carpenter. "Some of us, lad, are all for laying our hands on some riches before we dock. The hold is full of spices and gold ingots. Some of the passengers are laden with jewels.

We mean to steal the treasure and make off with it. There's quite a few islands around here we can hide on till the fuss blows over."

"You mean you're turning pirate?" gasped Hans.

"Turn pirate, aye. What do you say, lad? Will you join us? Many of us knew your father well and it's out of respect for him that I invite ye."

"My father is a law-abiding man," Hans protested. "He would never turn pirate, and neither would I!"

Just then there was a loud thud on the deck above. The battle between the pirates and the men still loyal to the first mate, the new captain, had begun. The fight was fierce but, in the end, the pirates won. They locked the captain in his cabin, pushing the surgeon and the quarter-master in with him. The wealthy passengers were stripped of their jewellery and money. The chests in the hold were smashed open and the pirates made away with the gold ingots and spices.

Two boats were lowered into the water, one filled with treasure, the other with provisions for the pirates. The wicked men climbed down into it one by one.

"'Tis a pity you won't join us, Hans, lad," called out the carpenter, who was bringing up the rear. "'Tis but a short journey to Davy Jones's Locker you be taking." And he hurled a lighted torch at the main-mast.

The sails caught fire right away. The passengers ran about the ship in a panic, screaming and wringing their hands. Hans, who had freed the first mate and his men, joined a chain gang pulling buckets of water out of the sea.

The wind was strong that night and the burning ship hurtled towards the coast of New England with alarming speed. It ran aground on Block Island, the hull splintering on the rocky shore.

Hans, and many others who could swim, dived into the icy water and clambered ashore. The locals rushed out to help in their hundreds, carrying wounded passengers ashore, giving out food and hot milk.

At sunrise the tide turned, dragging the burning ship back out to sea. Hans stood on the rocks and watched it disappear into the morning mist. It was a sad loss, but at least everyone on board had been saved. No lives had been lost.

Hans returned safely home on another schooner and grew up to be a fine sea captain. No one ever found out what became of the pirates and their stolen treasure. As for *The Palatine*, well, people on Block Island still glimpse her ghostly shape far out at sea on stormy nights. Her fiery sails light up the sky. It is said she appears to remind people of her tragic end long ago . . . .

Dogs to the Rescue
A STORY FROM RUSSIA

 A British gentleman called Mr Rappoport was on a journey through the Ural Mountains in a *troika*, a large sleigh with three horses. He'd been travelling for days, he was chilled to the bone and all he could do, as the sleigh trundled through a dark forest, was snooze under a warm blanket.

It was close to midnight when Ivan, the sleigh driver, woke him up. "Sir, do you hear that?"

Rappoport sat up in his seat. He could hear a faint howling in the darkness around him. "Is it wolves?" he asked.

"I'm afraid so," said Ivan.

"They sound too far away to catch up with us."

"The horses are tired, sir," said Ivan. "And hungry wolves run very fast. We must reach the lake before them. If they overtake us . . . "

The driver cracked his whip and the sleigh rocked on its large runners. The horses neighed. Rappoport reached for the rifle in his carpet bag. The howling grew louder and Rappoport became aware of red eyes, glaring in the dark behind him.

They sped on but, suddenly, the wolves were swarming around the sleigh, a sea of fur and gnashing jaws. Their sharp teeth were blindingly white in the dark, their eyes as red as coals.

The horses reared in fear. Ivan lashed out at the wolves with his whip.

"Get away! Get away, you brutes."

Rappoport aimed his rifle at the wolf closest to the horses and fired. It fell, but another beast took its place immediately. Rappoport fired again and again but his few bullets were nothing against that heaving ocean of snapping jaws. Soon the bullets ran out. Rappoport started lashing out at the wolves with the butt of his rifle. From the corner of his eye he saw one of them catch up with the horses. They were doomed . . . .

Then Rappoport heard another sound above the howling of the wolves. The barking of dogs! Mountain dogs! The wolves must have heard them too, for suddenly they stopped lunging at the horses and their ears pricked up.

The dogs, a whole pack of them, streamed out of the woods, their white fur glistening like snow in the darkness. Yapping at the wolves, they surrounded the sleigh. The wolves did not put up a fight but fell back, growling, their fur standing on end.

The last Rappoport saw of them, they were standing shoulder to shoulder on the mountain pass, their eyes glowing red with rage.

The hounds remained with the sleigh, protecting the horses. Rappoport reached out to stroke the one closest to him but it always seemed to be just out of reach and his fingers grasped nothing but thin air.

"You saved our lives, and our horses," he whispered. "How can we thank you enough?" He remembered he had some chocolate in his bag. He fished it out and threw it to the dogs.

Lights appeared up ahead. They were coming to the village on the shores of the lake. The dogs fell back, panting from their long run. Rappoport held up his hand in salute, but the mountain mist closed around them and the dogs were hidden from view.

* * *

Later that night, Rappoport recounted his story to the locals at the lakeside inn.

"You say you were asleep when the sleigh driver first heard the wolves?" said one of them. "Then you must have dreamt the whole thing. No one keeps hounds around here."

"But I assure you, we were rescued by dogs," insisted Rappoport.

"The mountain air is so thin it often plays tricks on the mind," added the landlord. "People imagine all sorts of things when they're up there. I remember a shepherd who swore he'd seen a Roman army feasting on barley bread. A Roman army in Russia! Can you imagine?"

Rappoport paid for his meal and went up to his room. 'Could I have imagined it all?' he wondered. 'It does seem fanciful now that I am safely in a lodging house. Perhaps the landlord is right. The mountain air did play a trick on me. No ghostly dogs came to my rescue.'

During the night, he had a vivid dream. The window in his room slid open, and one of the hounds leapt in. It bounded onto the bed, growled gently for a moment, and left again.

When Rappoport woke up in the morning, he found something on his pillow. It was the bar of chocolate he had thrown to the dogs!

I'll Be Back!
A STORY FROM LITHUANIA

 Rasa and her family lived in a tall old house. Rasa slept on the ground floor in the kitchen, her brother Johan slept on the first floor and her parents had an old metal bed in the attic.

One night Rasa's father was away, buying sheep in the big city. It was the beginning of winter and the air had turned suddenly icy. Cold enough to snow for the first time.

Rasa was in her cot by the fire, trying to get warm, when she heard someone rattling the front door. "It's locked," she shouted. "Go away or I'll fetch my mama. She'll be at you with the rolling pin."

"Your mama, eh?" replied a horrible voice that sounded like someone speaking through a mouthful of tar. "I'm going, never fear. But I'll be back! What's mine is mine and no one will take it from me."

Rasa was too scared to sleep in the kitchen after that. She carried her bedding upstairs and laid it out on Johan's bed, which was big enough to take the two of them. The next night she was trying to sleep, when she heard someone coming up the stairs. *Thump! Thump! Thump!* Clear as a mountain bell! Johan was fast asleep next to her, his head buried under the pillow.

"Go away, whoever you are," shouted Rasa. "I've got my big brother with me and he'll take a stick to you."

"Your big brother, eh?" moaned the voice, sounding even more horrible than the night before. "I'm going, never fear. But I'll be back! What's mine is mine and no one's going to take it away from me."

The next morning, Papa came back home with four new sheep for the farm. Rasa told him all about the intruder, but he only laughed and ruffled her hair.

"I think you've been reading too many scary fairy tales," he said. "How can anyone come in if the door is locked?"

Still, that night, Rasa begged to sleep in the attic with her parents. It was bitterly cold; the north wind was sweeping down the nearby mountains, piling snow against the house.

Her parents fell asleep the moment they got into bed but Rasa lay awake, listening. She could hear muffled footsteps on the ground floor. *Thump! Thump! Thump!* Across the kitchen floor they went, and up the stairs past Johan's room. *Thump! Thump! Thump!* Clear as a mountain bell!

Rasa shook her parents awake. "Ma, Pa, he's coming."

Now the footsteps were trudging up to the attic. *Thump! Thump! Thump!*

"Go away, whoever you are," Rasa shouted. "I've got my papa here with me and he'll take his shepherd's crook to you."

"Your papa, eh?" replied the voice. "If your papa is in there with you, I'm not going away. It's him I want to have it out with. What's mine is mine and no one will take it away from me."

The knob on the door started turning slowly.

Papa leapt across the room. He grabbed the doorknob in his hands to stop the door from opening. "What do you want?" he shouted.

"I want my boots," came back the reply. "I can't lie in the ground without them. It's freezing out there."

"Go back to your resting place," Papa shouted. "I promise we'll return your boots in the morning. Go away . . . Grandpa."

The doorknob stopped jiggling. The footsteps receded and Rasa turned to look at her father.

"Was that . . . Grandpa?"

Papa nodded. "I removed his boots just before we buried him last month. Your mother and I thought it a terrible waste to leave them on him. Such an expensive pair of leather boots! We decided Johan could have them when he was old enough. How were we to know Grandpa would miss them?"

The very next morning, Rasa and her family drove to the cemetery in the cart. Snow lay thick on the ground, covering Grandpa's grave.

Papa opened a saddlebag and pulled out a pair of shining boots. He placed them on the grave, right next to each other.

"Here they are, Grandpa," he said. "Mama gave them a good polishing, one last time."

"What's mine is mine," echoed a quavery voice. "No one's going to take it away from me." And then two wrinkled hands reached out of the snow and grabbed the boots, pulling them down into the grave.

"Rest in peace, Grandpa," called out Rasa before they all returned to the cart.

There was a chuckle from the grave. "Goodbye, lass. You're a brave one, to be sure. Just like your old Grandpa, heh-heh!"

That night Rasa had a dream. She was in the shed looking for something when Grandpa came in, all smiles, his eyes bright with mischief. He winked at Rasa and pointed to an old chest in the corner of the shed. And then he disappeared!

In the morning, Rasa went to the shed and looked in the chest. It was full of old things that Grandpa had used: bits of string, an old pipe, a penknife and a tin of shoe polish, all rusted with age. Rasa opened the tin and there, lying on top of the caked shoe polish, was a gold coin!

It was a present from Grandpa, for helping to return his beloved boots!

The Ghosts Who Danced

A STORY FROM IRELAND

Once there was a boy called Patrick who loved playing football. One evening he was taking a shortcut through a graveyard and what did he see? An old skull lying in the grass, for all the world like a football. Before he knew it, he'd raised his right foot and sent it flying. *Thwack!* The skull hit a gravestone and was smashed to bits.

All at once, a bony hand shot out of a nearby grave and grabbed Patrick by the ankle. "Kick a poor fellow when he's down, why don't ye?" hissed a voice in his ear, and the hand started dragging him deeper into the grave.

As luck would have it, old Father Robert happened to be crossing the graveyard. He sprinkled Patrick's leg with holy water and the skeleton let go. But that wasn't the end of the story. Every time Patrick tried to kick a ball, an invisible hand grabbed him by the ankles and held him fast. A ghostly voice whispered in his ear, "I will thwart you so, son, each time you try to kick something." And he did!

Patrick's dream of becoming a footballer lay in tatters. To cheer him up, his mother bought him a fiddle, and Patrick turned out to be as good at fiddling as he had been at football. Very soon he was in demand all over the county, to play his fiddle at parties and weddings and funerals.

Now, one night — Halloween night it was — Patrick was returning home late from a Christening. It was raining and he was soaked to the skin.

"I'll rest awhile," said Patrick to himself, and he sat under a big tree in a graveyard.

Just then it struck midnight. The graves all around him yawned open and the ghosts of the dead climbed out.

"Be you the fiddler we hired?" asked one of them, glaring at Patrick with eyes as dark as the soot in the devil's chimney.

"He must have been held up," replied Patrick. "There is no one here but me and I happen to be sheltering from the rain."

"I see you have a fiddle," said the dead man. "Are ye any good?" And he rattled a thick gold chain around his neck. He'd been the town mayor before he died.

"As good as the rest of them," said Patrick humbly.

"Will you play for us, then?" asked the ghost of the mayor. "It is Halloween night and we must dance. If you're good, we'll make it worth your while."

"Yes, play for us," roared the other ghosts, and they crowded round Patrick, chilling him to the bone.

Patrick put the bow to his fiddle and started playing right there in the rain. The ghosts danced merrily, leaping and jigging and twisting around the graves. The ones who had arms clapped in time to the music, and the ones who had heads on their necks whooped with joy.

When a rooster crowed in a nearby field, the ghosts shuffled to a stop. Their one night of freedom a year was over. They jostled around Patrick.

"You are good," they whispered.

"Very good indeed."

"The best Halloween we've ever had."

One of them reached into his pocket and tossed a handful of gold coins into Patrick's cap. The others did the same, and soon Patrick's cap was full to the brim with coins and jewellery.

The ghost of the mayor grinned, showing rotting teeth in his skull. "We promised you a rich reward." And he put his thick gold chain round Patrick's neck. "Don't forget to come back next year!" Then, laughing, he leapt back into his grave. The other ghosts retreated into theirs and the earth closed above their heads.

* * *

Patrick ran all the way home to share the good news with his mother. "But you mustn't tell anyone how I came into so much wealth, Ma," he said. "I promised the ghosts I will return next Halloween, and there'll be more treasure waiting for me, to be sure."

Ma promised, but it's not easy to keep a secret in a small village. Before long everyone was talking about Patrick's new clothes and Patrick's new horse. The poor woman could hardly leave the house without someone wanting to know how her son had obtained so much money so quickly.

One boy in particular kept pestering her day in day out. His name was Frank and he was an apprentice to the village baker.

Rumour had it that Frank was a liar and a cheat, and that he put chalk dust in his cakes out of sheer spite for his customers.

But Patrick's ma didn't see a cheat standing in front of her whenever he talked to her. She saw a little boy, very much like her own son, whose mother was always ill and unable to work.

"I know your mother is poorly," she said, "and that you have no money for medicine."

"We need money for heating too, and we owe the butcher for a month. My poor ma can only take beef broth. If only I had the good luck your Patrick had, I would be able to buy it for her every day."

"Do you know that old graveyard on the hill?" said Patrick's ma, whispering so no one would hear. "Patrick went there on Halloween with his fiddle and played for the ghosts. They rewarded him with gold and jewellery."

"So that's his secret, is it?" said Frank. "Thank you kindly. I'll not let anyone know what you told me."

It was nearly Halloween again and Frank was determined to get his hands on the ghosts' treasures himself. He bought a cheap fiddle – the cheapest he could find. And a big cap – the largest they had in the shop.

On Halloween night he approached Patrick, who was eating alone at the local tavern. "Going anywhere special tonight?" he asked.

"I'm playing at a Halloween party," replied Patrick. "Out of town."

"I've a journey to make tonight too," said Frank. "Brr, it's cold enough out there to freeze the strings off a fiddle. Let's have a drink to warm us up before we leave. My treat!"

He fetched wine from the bar and, when Patrick was not looking, slipped a sleeping potion into his glass. His ruse worked, and at midnight the ghosts discovered Frank and not Patrick under the tree in

the graveyard.

"Is last year's fiddler not coming?" roared the ghost of the mayor.

"I'm afraid he's unavailable," replied Frank. "He sent me in his place."

"But are you any good?" asked the mayor.

"If you're good, we'll make it worth your while," laughed the other ghosts.

"I am the best there is," said Frank.

In truth, he had not even bothered tuning up the fiddle. He tucked it under his chin and started playing. A sound like the howling of a cat in great pain echoed around the graveyard.

The ghosts stopped in mid-step, their eyes wide with shock.

"You said you were good," said the ghost of the mayor.

"The best," added the others.

"Put that instrument away," hissed the mayor. "You must be the worst fiddle player in the world."

"Oh no," cried the other ghosts. "This is the one night in the year when we're allowed to come out of our graves. Let him play on, terrible as he is."

Frank played and the ghosts stumbled around the graves, wincing at the awful sound of the cheap fiddle. The ones who had hands danced with them over their ears.

When the cock crowed, the ghosts crowded round Frank and filled his large cap with gold.

"Thank you," called Frank, as they all climbed back into their graves and the earth closed over them.

He ran all the way home, leaving the cheap fiddle under the tree. "Look, Ma," he said. "We're rich."

But when he looked in his cap, the gold had turned to rotten teeth.

* * *

As for Patrick, he returned to the graveyard the following Halloween and earned more gold. I guess he's playing for his friends there still. For Patrick died a long time ago and was buried with his fiddle in the churchyard on the hill.

The Haunted Farmhouse
A STORY FROM DEVON IN ENGLAND

When Albert's mother lost her job in the kitchen of a wealthy duchess, she and her two children moved to a farm. Downhouse, it was called, and a gloomy, dilapidated place it was too. Almost a ruin! The ceilings in the main house hung low and harboured spiders, the windows were small and every door and floorboard creaked.

The only thing in the place that worked properly was an old water pump in the yard. It had a stone base, decorated with a ring of small, glaring monsters.

"I bet you this place is haunted," said Abigail, Albert's big sister.

"Don't you go filling Albert's head with nonsense," snapped her mother. "We have enough trouble on our hands as it is." But she neglected to say that they had rented the place cheap because no one else wanted to live in it.

The first night they spent in the house, the children went to bed early, but they were too excited to sleep. Abigail, who was good at telling stories, was reading to Albert when they heard the sound of moaning. It was right outside the door, on the landing.

"Mama?" called Albert. There was no answer, but the floorboards creaked and footsteps echoed down the stairs. The front door opened and slammed shut again.

Albert and Abigail went to the window and peeped out. The moon was bright and they could quite clearly see a tall figure crossing the yard. It seemed to be a man dressed entirely in black.

He made for the water pump and stood there looking at it for a few moments. He shook his head, seemed to kick at the stone base angrily, and then walked right through the wall of an old, disused cowshed behind it.

"I was right after all," said Abigail. "This place is haunted."

Her mum, who had heard the eerie noise but not looked out of the window, agreed. "But we can't move out, even though the apparition scares me," she said. "I took a year's lease on the farm, so we're stuck with it. We'll just have to make sure we don't come into contact with the awful thing. If a ghost sees you, it might take a liking to your mortal soul. You'd be doomed to become its companion for evermore."

So the three of them took to going to bed well before eleven, to make sure they never came across the ghost. The mother made sure the children had everything they could possibly need during the night in their room: a jug of water, fruit, books to read, extra candles and a chamber pot.

Months passed and they almost got used to the ghost, even though they were still scared of it. They could hear it roaming the place on wintry nights, howling in the dark or cursing angrily.

* * *

Then, one night in spring, Albert fell ill. His brow grew hot and he kept asking for water.

"There is no more water," said Abigail at last. "I'm sorry, but you drank every last drop."

"Water," repeated Albert hoarsely.

"What are we to do?" Mother fretted. "Albert desperately needs water to cool him down but it's nearly eleven. If we leave the room we run the risk of bumping into that infernal ghost."

"I think it's not quite eleven yet," said Abigail. "If I hurry, I might make it to the pump and back before it appears."

"God bless you, child," said her mother. "You are a brave girl."

Abigail wasn't so sure she was brave. Her hands were trembling as she picked up the jug. Mother opened the door for her and she slipped out on to the landing. It was pitch dark. The floorboards creaked under her feet.

Abigail tiptoed towards the stairs. She was halfway down when she fancied she heard footsteps behind her. Her heart missed a beat. She broke into a run and opened the front door, leaving it wide open as she crossed the yard to the pump.

She was reaching for the lever when a hand came down on her shoulder. "Let me help you, Miss."

Abigail jumped. She turned and there behind her was the man in black. The ghost!

"Please, don't run away," whispered the ghost, and a tear ran down his cheek. "I am tired of wandering around this farm. I want to rest in peace. Please accept my help."

"I accept," said Abigail.

"Thank you," said the ghost. He worked the lever on the pump and water poured into the jug.

"You have set me free," the ghost said to Abigail when the jug was full. "I owned this farmstead once. Swimming in gold I was, and a miser. I never helped anyone, not even my own workers. When I passed away, I was condemned to walk the earth until I was kind to someone. And now I have helped you. I am free."

"May your soul rest in peace, sir," whispered Abigail, picking up the jug.

"You shall have a reward," said the ghost. "The stone base under this pump is hollow. If you break it open, you will find my treasure. I buried it there when I was still alive. Use it to bring this farm back to life. Your family will prosper here. And make sure you are kind to people less fortunate than you."

"I will," Abigail promised.

The ghost smiled, lifted his face to the moon, and a moment later he had melted away.

Abigail carried the jug indoors to Albert, who drank deeply and then fell into a peaceful sleep.

In the morning she walked to a nearby village and fetched a stonemason. The lad broke open the stone base under the pump, where Abigail found a small chest full of gold coins.

Her mother used the treasure to repair the farm, and many people from all around came to work on it. Abigail was kind and generous to them all, rich or poor. Just as she had promised the ghost!

Them Bananas!

A STORY FROM EAST AFRICA

Once there were two brothers called Mahimbwa and Kibwana. They often went walking in the forest, and they always came back home with tasty vegetables for the cooking pot or wild fruit for breakfast. The boys were orphans and had to look after themselves, although everyone in the village kept an eye on them.

One day the boys came across a grizzled old banana tree. It had a hollow trunk, with a hole so big you could stick your head in it. They were both hungry, so Mahimbwa, who was the tallest, picked the bananas and Kibwana peeled them. When they'd eaten, Mahimbwa buried the peel in the ground while Kibwana thanked the forest spirit for her generosity.

That night, when the brothers were in their hammocks, there was a knock on the door of their hut. A voice wailed, "Them bananas you stole were mine. Give me back my bananas, or you'll be sorry."

Both boys sat up at once and there, glaring at them through the bars of the window, was a hideous creature with flaming red eyes. Nearly every tooth in its mouth was missing and instead of hair on its head there was dried grass crawling with glowworms.

"We didn't know they were anybody's bananas," called Mahimbwa. "We're sorry! Now go away."

But the hideous creature did not leave. It started flinging banana peel through the window and it did not stop till the sun came up.

It took the boys all morning to clean the hut. That night, before they went to bed, Kibwana put a storm shutter in the window and Mahimbwa made sure it was fastened properly.

Round about midnight, the wind picked up and someone knocked at the door again. The hideous creature's voice wailed, "Them bananas were mine. Give me back my bananas or you'll be sorry."

"We told you we didn't know they were your bananas," cried Kibwana. "We're sorry. Now leave us in peace."

But the creature just laughed a rasping laugh and, despite the door and window being shut, the boys were pelted with bones. By morning they were covered in bruises.

Kibwana insisted they go and see the doctor.

"It seems you have angered a tree ghost, a *majini*," said the doctor, when he heard their story. "You mustn't stay at home tonight. If the tree ghost finds you again, I fear he will throw more than bones. He will throw rocks big enough to crush your heads. Bring your hammocks to my hut. You'll be safe here."

The boys went home for their hammocks, locking the door behind them when they left, to make sure the tree ghost could not get in and wreck the house. That night, before they all went to bed, the doctor turned the key in the door and his wife put storm shutters in all the windows.

On the stroke of midnight it started to rain. Thunder rolled in the hills and the wind howled like a wounded lion chasing a hunter. Suddenly there was a knock on the door, and the tree ghost moaned, "Them bananas you stole were mine. Give me back my bananas or you'll be sorry."

The doctor called out from his hammock, "They can't give you your bananas back. They ate them and have them no more. Go back to your tree and tomorrow we'll bring you a treat much nicer than bananas."

Thunder rolled again and the wind howled louder and longer. The tree ghost rattled the doorknob. "I shall go, but if your treat is not nicer than my bananas I will throw more than bones at you tomorrow . . . ."

By morning the rain had stopped and the sky was clear. The doctor and the boys went out to the forest, taking a cooking pot and a ladle with them. When they got to the banana tree, the doctor lit a fire and put water and cornmeal porridge in the pot. He sent Kibwana to find some wild honey, and Mahimbwa to gather peanuts. The porridge

thickened. The doctor stirred in Kibwana's honey and Mahimbwa added the crushed peanuts.

"Now that is a treat no one can resist," said the doctor. "Let's hope your ghost likes it." And he led the boys home, leaving the porridge pot under the tree.

* * *

That night the boys could not sleep for fear the tree ghost might return. Mahimbwa read a story, while Kibwana whittled at a stick.

On the stroke of midnight, the wind started to rise, hissing like a snake closing in on its prey. The boys heard someone shuffling up to the door and a voice whispered, "Them bananas you stole were mine, but the porridge you gave me was creamy, the honey was sweet and the nuts were crunchy. I forgive you, but never steal my bananas again. I'll want something tastier than porridge next time . . . ."

Then the boys heard something hitting the doorstep with a loud clang. In the morning, they found the tree ghost had returned the doctor's cooking pot and ladle. The boys washed them and dried them, and from then on they were careful never to pick fruit from a tree with a hollow trunk!

Welcome to the Red Palace Inn
A STORY FROM CHINA

Wang the messenger needed money badly, so when a magistrate paid him to deliver a letter to his brother in the city, he set off right away.

That night, a fierce wind began to blow. It started to rain. Wang was on a dark country road but, looking round for shelter, he spotted a light high up on a hill. Thinking it might be coming from a farm, he ran to it.

The building he found was not a farm. It was a wayside inn, large as a castle. Torches were burning on either side of the entrance. Above the gate hung a sign with huge gold letters.

WELCOME TO THE RED PALACE INN.
Softest beds and freshest fried pork in the district

Wang slipped through the door and found himself in a large hall, its crimson walls decorated with tapestries. An old man in a white cap and smock hurried up to him. "I am afraid we have no vacancies tonight, sir," he said.

"I have come a long way," said Wang. "My feet are swollen from walking on the hard road. Can you not find me a room? The smallest one will do."

A stout man, holding a meat cleaver, appeared behind the first one.

40

"We are holding a great banquet tonight. A hundred fierce warriors are on their way, expecting to eat. We have no extra food or wine. You'd best be on your way."

"I need no wine or meat," said Wang. "Just a cup of hot green tea will do."

The man in the white cap whispered something to the stout one, who was obviously the cook. The cook made a face, but the man in the cap smiled at Wang. "It is true we have no food or wine to spare but the storm is getting heavier out there. You cannot spend the night outside. The kitchen boy is away tonight, visiting his sick mother. You can have his room for only a yen."

Wang was shown to a tiny room overlooking the yard. There was no bed, only a bamboo carpet on the floor. Wang stretched out on it and, using his damp cloak for a pillow, fell asleep right away.

Some time later he was woken up by a loud noise. He could hear shouting, and the sound of hoofbeats. Peeping through a crack in the door, he saw the yard filling up with warriors on horseback. They were magnificent, all dressed in red tunics, with helmets on their heads. Their beards flowed down to their chests.

The man in the white cap bowed low to them.

"Greetings," he said. "Everything is ready for you."

The warriors climbed off their horses and most of them hurried into the crimson hall at the end of the yard. The smell of cooked pork and sweet, heavy sauce filled the air. Wang heard the warriors sitting down to their meal. The sound of their laughter carried on the wind.

Then a young man in an officer's uniform ran across the yard and shouted, "The general is coming. The general is coming."

The iron gate was pulled wide open, and Wang saw two lines of young boys enter, each boy holding a red paper lantern on a pole. There was the thundering of beating hooves, and the general's horse came charging through the gate. The general climbed down and, handing a large wooden shield to the young officer, followed the man in the white cap to the hall. The sound of his warriors greeting him shook the walls.

Wang had never seen a general up close but now was his chance. What a tale to tell his friends back home! He crept out of his room and stole through the empty kitchen to the great hall. None of the warriors noticed him as he squeezed behind a tapestry to watch the feast. At last the general stood up and wiped his long beard on a silken napkin.

"This old corpse is ready for bed," he announced. "But you men go on feasting. We shall not taste delicious food like this again for a long time. Tomorrow we have a harsh battle ahead of us."

The warriors raised their wine cups to the general.

"Victory or death," they chanted. "Victory or death."

The young officer who'd taken the general's wooden shield went up

to him and led him out. Wang followed them down a dark corridor. He saw the young officer open a door and the general went in. Finding a hole in the wooden wall, Wang put his eye to it.

The only light in the room was a small lamp hanging from the ceiling. The general was lying on a cot. His hands were folded across his long white beard. The young officer removed his boots, putting them side by side at the door. He removed the general's helmet. The general turned his head . . . and his eyes locked into Wang's.

"Who's there?" he roared. "Arrest that man."

Wang gasped loudly. He leapt back from the hole in the wall, crashing into a large vase behind him. The sound of breaking china was deafening. Wang picked himself up and ran blindly down the corridor. He bolted across the yard and out through the iron gate.

An ox cart was coming down the road. Wang waved at the driver and the cart stopped. Wang clambered on to it, burrowing into the wet hay. He didn't come out again until the cart stopped outside another inn and the driver climbed down.

"Thank you for giving me a lift," said Wang, climbing down after him. "You saved my life."

The driver laughed. "You're welcome, my friend. But I hardly think a little rain was going to kill you."

"It wasn't the rain I was running away from," replied Wang. "It was the general at the inn."

"The inn?" said the driver, puzzled. "I saw you running down a bare hill. There is no other inn on the Beijing Road except this one."

Just then they were joined by another traveller. "I heard tell there used to be an inn further up the road," he said. "Mighty warriors were in the habit of meeting there for a feast before a battle. It burned down hundreds of years ago."

Wang stared at the traveller. "Do you know what the inn was called?"

"Oh yes," replied the traveller. "It was called . . . The Red Palace Inn."

The Guest

A STORY FROM BRAZIL

Miguel was having a midnight feast to celebrate his birthday, up in his tree house at the bottom of the garden. His mother made him rice and beans. His granny baked him honey cakes covered in thick dark chocolate.

"Now all I need are some ripe papayas," said Miguel to himself. "I'll make some nice cool papaya juice for my friends to drink."

There was a papaya tree just outside the village, and that's where Miguel went to get his fruit. He chose twelve of the ripest papayas and placed them carefully in his wicker basket.

Just as he was leaving, he spotted something among the broad papaya leaves that was much bigger than a fruit. It was a skull, stuck on a branch.

"Hello," said Miguel, who was always telling jokes. "You're a strange kind of papaya. Wouldn't want to bite into you. Ouch! I'd break my teeth on you."

He looked down at the ground and there was the rest of the skeleton, half hidden in the weeds. "Oh dear," groaned Miguel. "This guy talks so much his body is trying to get away from his mouth, ha ha!"

He stuck a finger in the hole where the skull's nose had been, and wiggled it. "There," he said to the skull. "I'm picking your nose for you. Isn't that nice of me? Pity you don't have legs any more, my friend. You could come to my midnight feast tomorrow, up in my tree house. I bet you're the life and soul of the party, ha ha." Then he pulled his fingers out of the skull's nose and went home.

Miguel had invited twelve people to the feast, all close friends from school. They arrived early, eager for the honey cakes, and Miguel sat them round in a circle. It was very late when they finished eating.

"Now for some papaya juice," said Miguel. "I made it myself with ripe papayas." He got up to fetch the pitcher.

Just then the church clock up the road struck midnight. There was a loud knock at the tree-house door and Miguel went to answer it. "That's odd," he said. "I don't remember inviting anyone else."

A tall, lean figure was standing in the darkness. It had a heavy black cloak on, and a hood covered its face completely.

"Good evening," whispered a voice under the hood. "Thank you for inviting me to your birthday party. May I come in?"

And the hooded figure swept into the house, the black cloak swirling around it. Miguel's friends all moved up to make space in the circle.

"May I take your coat?" Miguel asked the stranger, racking his brains to remember who else he'd invited to the party.

"I'll keep it on if you don't mind," hissed the new guest, and his voice echoed like a shout in a tomb.

"You're just in time to have a glass of fresh papaya juice with us," said Miguel, who for the first time in his life could not think of a single wisecrack to make. He filled a glass with juice and handed it to the stranger.

"*Salud*," said the guest in the hood. He raised the glass with gloved hands. Musty old gloves they were, full of holes and covered in mildew. There was a loud sucking noise as he drank, and papaya juice dribbled out of the hood, making a big yellow pool on the wooden floor.

"Are you all right?" asked Miguel. "Your . . . your mouth . . . seems to be leaking."

The hooded guest continued drinking and the pool of juice on the floor got bigger.

"Now . . . that . . . was . . . very . . . tasty," declared the guest, and he set the empty glass down.

"Forgive me for being so rude," said Miguel. "But may I ask who you are?"

"Don't you remember me?" replied the guest. "We met yesterday near the old papaya tree on the hill. You picked my nose for me, and you invited me to your party. Remember?" And he threw back the hood to reveal . . . a grinning skull.

Miguel and his friends got the shock of their lives. The skeleton roared with laughter and ran out of the door. The last Miguel saw of him he was flying through the air like a giant bat, his black cloak flapping all around him.

I can tell you, the poor boy never dared to be rude to anyone again after that.

The Ghost and his Uncle
A STORY FROM BENGAL IN INDIA

Once there was a kind barber, who worked very hard all day, shaving poor customers by the river.

His wife said, "What's the use of shaving people who can't afford to pay you? We're soon going to be penniless ourselves. I couldn't even afford to buy milk this morning."

"You're right," said the barber. "I need to find a better kind of customer." And he put all his barber's tools in a sack. "I'm going to the big city to seek my fortune, my dearest. You'll see – I'll come back a rich man."

"You'll no doubt end up shaving travellers on the road for free," replied his wife. "But go with my blessing." And she made him some tiffin to take with him.

The barber set off right away and, by sundown, reached a dark forest. He settled under a tree and opened the tiffin box to eat his rice and lentils. Well, the spicy smell of lentils woke up a forest ghost who was sleeping in a tree nearby.

The ghost was hungry too, and he fancied the barber for his dinner. He leapt out of his hiding place, roaring at the top of his voice.

The barber nearly dropped his tiffin box in surprise. He looked up and saw the ghost glaring at him. It had a green face, sharp teeth and

long bony fingers that wiggled.

"I've come to suck your blood," moaned the ghost.

The barber was terrified, but he kept calm. "You'll do no such thing," he replied. "One more word out of you and . . . and I'll put you in my sack. I'm a ghost catcher and I've got space for one more ghost."

The ghost, who was quite young, had been warned of ghost catchers by his uncle, the oldest ghost in the forest. Still, this man didn't look at all dangerous. "I don't believe you have ghosts in there," he said cheekily.

"Don't you?" said the barber, putting down his tiffin box. "I'll show you one, if you like." He reached into the sack and whipped out a mirror.

"There," he cried, holding it up to the ghost's face. "The poor fellow looks just like you, doesn't he? You'll be next, I'm warning you. All I have to do is chant a spell and you'll be in there with the others."

The ghost, who had never seen a mirror before, fell for the trick. "Please, please," he begged, "don't catch me. I'm a very powerful ghost and I have an uncle who is even more powerful. If you let me go, I'll grant you a wish. Two wishes! What do you say?"

"Since you're so generous, I'll let you go this time," said the barber. "But mind my wishes come true or I'll come after you with my spells."

"What are your wishes?" asked the ghost.

"For a start, I want a bag of gold right now," answered the barber. "And then I want you to build a barn right next to my house and fill it with sacks of lentils."

"Your wish is my command," said the ghost, bowing three times, and a bag of gold appeared at the barber's feet.

The barber picked it up and took it home.

His wife was overjoyed to see him and, when she saw the gold, she gave him a big hug.

"Did I not tell you I'd come back a rich man?" laughed the barber. He took his wife outside and there, where an empty field used to be, was a barn filled with sacks of lentils.

Now the young forest ghost really did have an uncle. He was even more hideous than his nephew, with a blue face and wispy hair that trailed down the back of his neck like cotton wool. The young ghost told him all about the barber and the uncle shook with rage.

"You let a silly man trick you," he said. "I'll wager he was no ghost catcher. Take me to him and we'll find out exactly how he managed to outwit you. Then I'll suck the blood right out of his neck."

The young ghost floated with his uncle to the barber's house. It was the middle of the night but the barber was still awake, thinking about all the wonderful things he could do with his gold. When the ghost's uncle peered through the window, the barber guessed right away what was happening.

Quick as a flash, he grabbed his sack off the floor and pulled out the mirror, making sure the ghost's uncle could see his own reflection in it.

"Here's another one for my sack," he bellowed. "I've got one like this already but it would be nice to have two."

The ghost's uncle, who also had never seen a mirror before, fell for the barber's trick, just like his nephew! He backed away from the window, wailing loudly.

"Please don't put me in your sack. I'm a very powerful ghost and I can make your wish come true. Two wishes!"

The barber smiled and said, "I've got all the gold and lentils I need but I'll let you go, if you grant me THREE wishes."

"It's a deal," groaned the ghost's uncle.

"First of all," said the barber, "I want a diamond necklace for my wife."

The ghost's uncle bowed three times and a diamond necklace appeared round the neck of the barber's wife.

"Next, I want you to build me another barn and fill it with sacks of rice," commanded the barber.

The ghost's uncle murmured a spell and the barn appeared behind him, right next to the first one. "And your last wish . . . ?" he asked the barber.

"My last wish," laughed the barber, "is that I am never bothered by you, your nephew or any other ghost ever again. *Dhonnobad!* Be gone!"

And both ghosts disappeared in a puff of awful-smelling smoke!

Atchoo!

A STORY FROM KOREA

A boy called Shin was on his way to the big city, to sit for an important exam. His mother had made him new clothes and baked a cake for him to take, but there was no money for hiring a donkey. Shin had to travel on foot.

He was going through wild country when he heard someone sneeze very loudly.

Atchoo!

Shin stopped and peered around him. He could see no one.

Atchoo!

There was the sound again! Shin looked to his left. He looked to his right. Still he could see no one.

"Hello?" called out Shin.

There was no answer, only the sound of the wind in the trees.

Shin was about to start walking again when he saw a grave by the side of the road. My, how dusty it looked. No one had cleaned it for weeks. And the carvings on it were all grimy. The flowers on the altar were dead.

"It is wrong to forget the dead," said Shin out loud. He made a broom from twigs and swept the grave until there was no more dust on it. He polished the carvings, he put wild flowers in the vase and, when he was ready to go, he left a piece of cake from his bundle on the altar. It wasn't a very big piece but it was an offering just the same, a mark of respect to the person buried in the forgotten grave.

When it got dark, Shin took shelter in a barn, nestling down to sleep on a mound of warm straw. It was a stormy night and the sound of thunder woke him up. Someone else had come into the barn while he was asleep, an old scholar dressed in flowing white robes with a cap on his head. His whiskers were long and plaited, and hung down to his chest. He was sitting on a bale of hay by the door.

"Good evening," said Shin. "Or is it good morning?"

"It is yet to get light," said the old man. "There is still time to rest. You will need to keep your wits about you in the big city tomorrow."

"What do you mean?" asked Shin.

"You are going to sit a very important exam, are you not?" replied the old man. "If you pass, you will be able to find a good position later on in life. You will be able to help your widowed mother."

"How do you know all this?" said Shin.

"I can see things which others cannot," said the old man. "Now listen to me very carefully. The exam will have two parts. The first task will be to write a poem. About clouds! That's to prove to your examiners that you can use your imagination. I have written one for you already. It goes like this:

Clouds
filling the sky
turn blue to grey

To the farmer
they bring rain
To the idle man in the park
they bring shadow

Your second task will be to describe the city and put forward ideas on how the lives of its citizens could be improved. That is to show your examiners that you can use your imagination for the common good. I have thought about the best way to answer this question . . . ."

And the old man explained to Shin what he should write. He smiled when he finished. "I trust you will remember all that. We must get a little sleep before morning." He lay on the floor, folded his arms across his chest and promptly started snoring.

When Shin woke up in the morning, the old man had already left. 'I think perhaps he was a little mad,' thought Shin as he walked into the city. 'Fancy thinking you can tell what's going to be in an exam.'

But when the city scholars gave out the exam papers, there were the two questions.

Part 1:   Please write a poem about clouds.

Part 2:   Please describe in your own words what you have seen of our city and how life could be improved for its inhabitants.

Shin wrote down every single word the mysterious man in the barn had told him. When the exam was over, he gave the scholars his papers and hurried away. He was eager to get back home to his mother.

Passing by the old grave again, he spotted a young woman placing lilies on the altar.

"Greetings," she said.

"Greetings," replied Shin. "Those are beautiful flowers."

"They were my grandfather's favourites," said the girl. "I try to keep his grave tidy as much as I can, but I've been ill these past few weeks. I worry when there's too much dust on the gravestone. My grandfather hated dust, and just a hint of it in the house used to make him sneeze alarmingly. When he was dying he joked with me. "Don't let the dust gather on my grave, Cho Hee, or it'll make me sneeze so." The girl laughed. "As if the dead can sneeze."

"Perhaps they can," said Shin.

"My grandfather was full of stories," said the girl. "But he was a wise man too, a teacher. 'If people are kind to you, Cho Hee,' he would say, 'make sure you help them in return.'" She opened a bag and drew out a little picture frame. "He had such a kind face, look."

Shin looked at the picture and there, smiling at him, was the very same man he'd met in the barn the night before! And when Shin arrived home, he found a message to say he had passed the exam – with flying colours!

About the Stories

THE GHOST SHIP

The much-loved legend of the 'Palatine Light' is based on a true incident. In 1738 a ship called *The Princess Augusta* was wrecked on Block Island in the state of Rhode Island in the USA. Most of its passengers were Germans from the Palatine region of Germany, so the ship eventually became known as *The Palatine*. Over the years there have been many different versions of the story. Mine is based on a description from *The History of Block Island* by Samuel Livermore, published in 1877, and William Gilmore Simm's *The Ship of the Palatines*, which first appeared in *The Ladies' Companion* magazine in 1843.

DOGS TO THE RESCUE

Animal ghosts are almost as frequent as human apparitions. People have reported sightings of phantom dogs, cats, horses, bulls, pigs, tigers, elephants and even apes. Most stories about domestic pets tend to show the ghosts as friendly creatures protecting people from real-life danger. 'Dogs to the Rescue' is believed to be a true story from Russia, based on a report published by Eliott O'Donnell in *Animal Hauntings* in 1913.

I'LL BE BACK!

Stories of ghosts that try to retrieve stolen possessions are popular all over the world. It is said that their spirits cannot rest until their worldly goods are returned to them. 'I'll Be Back!' is a typical example of this genre. I first read it in a collection of Lithuanian folklore compiled by Jonas Balys, and published in *Lithuanian Folk Legends About the Dead*, in 1951.

THE GHOSTS WHO DANCED

Irish folklore is rich in all kinds of ghosts, from phantom leprechauns to houses haunted by spectres of people who are not even dead yet. Many tend to have a wicked sense of humour, like the ghosts in this story. I first read it in *Legends of Kerry* by T. Crofton Croker and Sigerson Clifford, published in 1972.

THE HAUNTED FARMHOUSE

Britain is said to be one of the most haunted countries in the world. The city of York alone is believed to have more than 500 ghosts. Our story comes from Devon, a county rich in legend and spooky moors. I first read it in *Devon Traditions and Fairy Tales*, by JRW Coxhead, published in 1959.

THEM BANANAS!

In African folklore it's not just houses that can be haunted. Ghosts may lurk in caves, disused watering holes, wells and even hollow trees. The African people who speak a language called Bantu sometimes call ghosts *majini*. It's a word derived from the Arabic word *djinn*, meaning genie. I based my story on a legend from Alice Werner's *Myths and Legends of the Bantu*, published in 1933.

WELCOME TO THE RED PALACE INN

Ghost stories are very popular in China. There is even a Ghost Festival, held by Chinese communities around the world. No one dares move house during the festival or walk down a dark street alone, in case they are followed by ghosts. This story is based on a version from *The Chinese Fairy Book*, by R. Wilhelm Fredrick Stokes, published in 1921.

THE GUEST

Brazilian ghost stories are a mixture of native myths and old legends brought to the country by African and European immigrants. My story is based on a folk story found in *Brazilian Folktales*, by Livia Maria M de Almeida, Ana Maria Portella and Margaret Read MacDonald, published in 2006.

THE GHOST AND HIS UNCLE

Ghosts in India haunt all kinds of places, such as ruined palaces, forts, wells and abandoned villages. There is even a haunted beach, where people hear mysterious whispers carried on the sea-breeze. My story is taken from *Folk Tales of Bengal*, collected by Lal Behari Dey and first published in 1883.

ATCHOO!

Spooks in Korea tend to stick to abandoned houses, dark forests and graveyards. They are trapped there until they finish a task they started while alive. Others, like the one in this story, appear because they do not want to be forgotten. I found it in *Korean Folktales, Imps and Ghosts* by James S. Gale, published in 1913.